How to be a Pirate in 10 easy stages

Written and illustrated by Scoular Anderson

STAGE 1
What kind of pirate do you want to be?

To help you decide, here are some famous pirates.

A Terrifying Pirate
Blackbeard had
a long beard
which he tied
with ribbons.

A Wild Pirate
Anne Bonny had
a terrible temper.

A Sneaky Pirate
John Avery sailed off
with the treasure
belonging to other pirates.

A Gentleman Pirate
Bartholomew Roberts loved
fine clothes and only drank tea.

A Cunning Pirate
Captain and Mrs Cobham got up
to all sorts of clever tricks.

STAGE 2
Wear the right clothes

Pirate captains often wore smart clothes.

a tricorn hat

a silk waistcoat

lace cuffs

Cordoba boots with bucket tops

The sails of pirate ships were made of **canvas**. Ordinary pirates often had to use bits of canvas to make their clothes.

When their ship was sailing, the **crew** had to climb around the **rigging**. To make this easy, they wore baggy clothes and took off their shoes.

They wore earrings because they thought it made their eyesight better.

Pirates usually **plaited** their hair in a pigtail. Then the pigtail was covered in flour and water to make it stiff. Pirates wore all sorts of hats and headgear.

canvas hat

Monmouth cap

scarf

Jacobin cap

STAGE 3
Where to find your crew

The **inns** round **harbours** were full of sailors.
Many wanted to be pirates because it seemed
an exciting life. It was also very dangerous.

Often, when pirates attacked a ship, they forced
the crew from that ship to join them as pirates.

You're a pirate now, sir!

STAGE 4
What sort of ship do you need?

Here are some ships that pirates liked.

LUGGERS were small and fast.

CUTTERS were even smaller. They could hide in narrow creeks and bays.

SCHOONERS were easy to sail.

BRIGS were bigger but could change direction quickly.

7

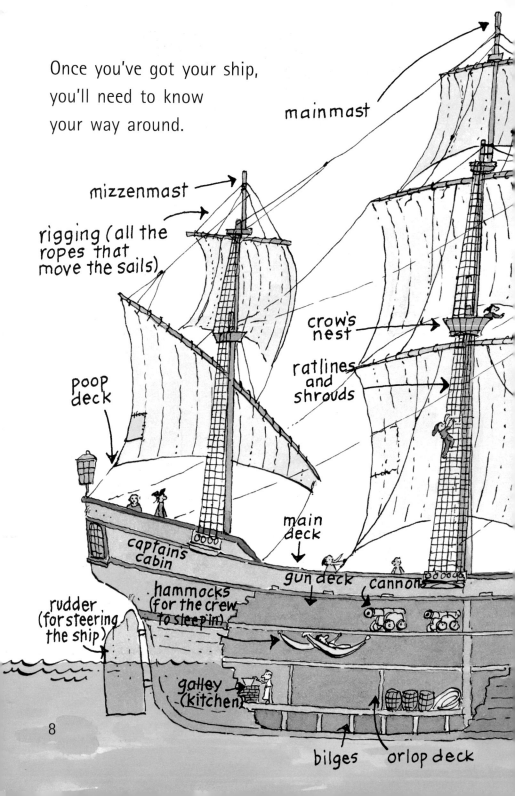

Once you've got your ship, you'll need to know your way around.

mainmast

mizzenmast

rigging (all the ropes that move the sails)

crow's nest

ratlines and shrouds

poop deck

main deck

captains cabin

gun deck

cannon

rudder (for steering the ship)

hammocks (for the crew to sleep in)

galley (kitchen)

bilges   orlop deck

8

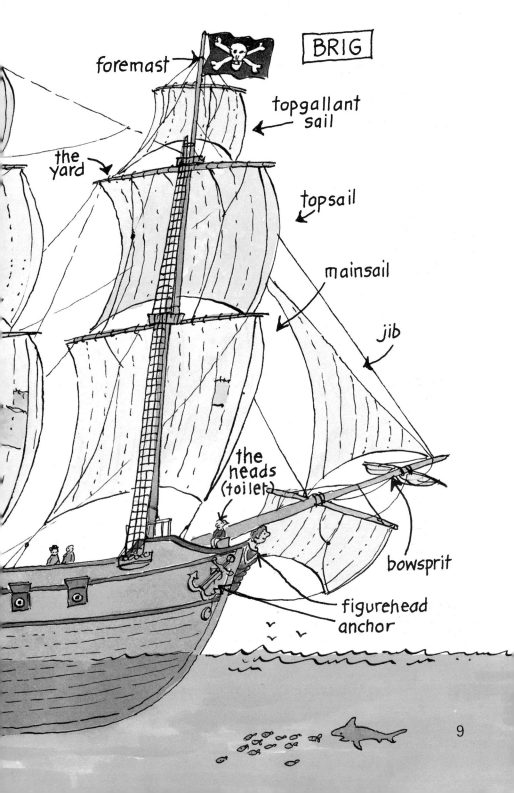

BRIG

foremast

topgallant
sail

the
yard

topsail

mainsail

jib

the
heads
(toilet)

bowsprit

figurehead
anchor

9

STAGE 5
Where to be a pirate

Pirates sailed everywhere, but their favourite place was the Caribbean Sea.

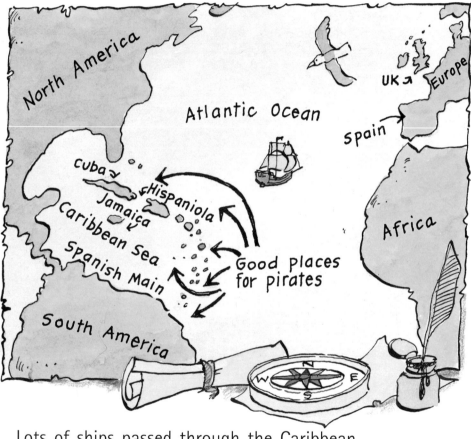

Lots of ships passed through the Caribbean.
They carried gold and silver from
South America to Europe.

The Caribbean was full of islands that were
good hiding places for pirates.

Barbecue is a Caribbean word. Pirates had
barbecues while they waited for a ship to attack.

STAGE 6
Keep your crew happy

Food on board a pirate ship wasn't very nice.

This is what pirates ate most of the time:

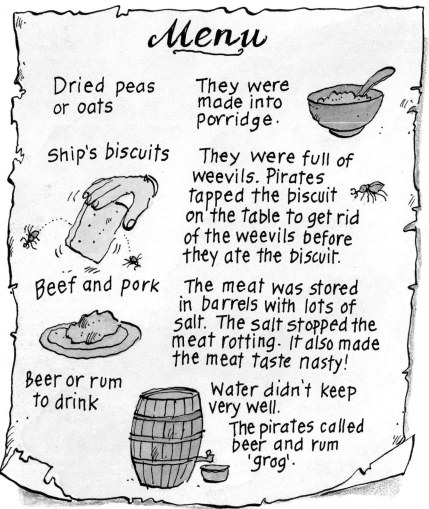

Menu

Dried peas or oats
They were made into porridge.

Ship's biscuits
They were full of weevils. Pirates tapped the biscuit on the table to get rid of the weevils before they ate the biscuit.

Beef and pork
The meat was stored in barrels with lots of salt. The salt stopped the meat rotting. It also made the meat taste nasty!

Beer or rum to drink
Water didn't keep very well. The pirates called beer and rum 'grog'.

Once a week the pirates had a day off. It was called a "make and mend day". This was when pirates washed and mended their clothes or had a haircut.

They were also allowed to dance and sing. They played musical instruments and games like cards and **dice**.

STAGE 7
Don't let the crew cause trouble

If pirates misbehaved on the ship,
they had to be punished.

A pirate might get 40 lashes
with the cat-o'-nine-tails.
The cat was a whip made
with knotted ropes.

A pirate might be put down in
the bilges – the lowest, darkest
part of the ship. It was very damp
and smelly down there. The pirate's
legs were tied to an iron bar
called the bilboes.

A pirate might get
ducked at the
yardarm. He would
be tied to a rope and
ducked in the sea
several times.

STAGE 8
Fly the right flag

When the pirates spotted a ship,
they tried to find out which
country it came from.

They're flying the Spanish flag, Captain.

Then the pirates flew the same flag. This was a trick because it made the other ship think the pirates were friends. This allowed the pirate ship to sail closer to its victim.

They're friendly, sir. They're flying the Spanish flag.

If the pirates flew a white flag it meant **"Surrender!"**

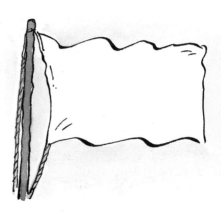

If they flew a red flag it meant "We're going to turn nasty!"

If they flew a black flag it meant "We're going to attack!"

The black flag was called the Jolly Roger. Sometimes it had a skull or skeleton painted on it.

STAGE 9
Attack!

When the pirates attacked a ship, this is what they did.

First, the cannons were fired.

How to fire a cannon

1. Put a cartridge of gunpowder and a cannonball into the cannon.

2. Push them right to the bottom of the cannon.

3. Prick a hole in the cartridge.

4. Light the gunpowder.

5. FIRE!

BLAM!

6. Clean the inside of the cannon and start again.

Then the pirates threw grappling irons. The irons caught hold of the ship. The pirates climbed up the ropes that were tied to the irons.

They jumped over the side of the ship.

They waved their **pistols** and **cutlasses** and made a terrifying noise.

WAARGH!

WHOOH!

19

STAGE 10
What to do with the treasure

There might be gold, silver and precious stones on board the ship that had been attacked.

There might be money. In those days, the money had names like doubloons, sequins, guineas and pieces of eight.

There might be cargo to sell, like fine cloth, spices or china.

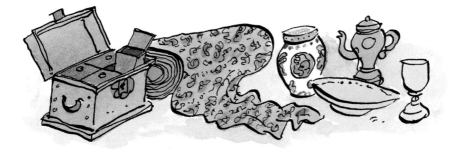

Pirates didn't often bury their treasure on desert islands. They usually sailed to the nearest harbour to spend their money!

Some pirates saved their money, because even pirates wanted to live happily ever after. So, do you think you want to be a pirate?

GLOSSARY

barbecue a grill on which food is cooked outdoors over an open fire, or hot charcoal

canvas a strong cloth, used for making sails

crew the people who work on a ship

cutlasses curved swords

dice a game where two people roll, then show their dice, and the one with the highest score wins

harbours areas of deep water where boats can stay safely

inns small hotels

pistols small guns

plaited twisting three strands of hair over each other in turn

rigging the ropes, cables and chains on a ship

surrender to give up

yardarm the end of the wooden pole that holds up a sail

INDEX

Ideas for guided reading

Learning objectives: Posing questions before reading non-fiction and finding answers; reading and understanding challenging words; using contents page and index to find way about text.

Curriculum links: Geography: Island Home, Where in the world is Barnaby Bear?; History: Why do we remember famous people?

Interest words: terrifying, misbehaved, surrender, precious

Resources: Small dry wipe boards and pens

Word count: 1092

Getting started

This book can be read over two sessions.

- Read the title and look through the book. Allow time for the children to enjoy the illustrations and humorous structure of the text.

- Read pp2–3. Discuss the fact that even though this book makes us laugh it has lots of interesting information about pirates.

- Focus on the contents page. Ask the children to write down a question about pirates e.g. Why did pirates fly different flags? Model finding the right page and then answering this question.

- Scan through the book together. Point out that the chapter headings could be useful in designing questions, and that there are many useful ways of presenting information in this book – instructions, maps, glossary, diagrams etc. Also point out the text '…is in the past tense' – because traditional pirates lived many years ago.

Reading and responding

- Model to children how to read multi-syllabic words by finding parts of the words they know or clapping the separate syllables. They should then reread the sentence and check that it sounds right and makes sense.